I Like Myself!

Karen Beaumont

Illustrated by David Catrow

Harcourt, Inc.
Orlando Austin New York San Diego Toronto London

Wishing every child the magic of self-acceptance and love—K. B.

To Jeannette, for pushing me outside the envelope—D. C.

For information about permission to reproduce selections from this book, write to
trade.permissions@hmhco.com or to Permissions, Houghton Mifflin Harcourt
Publishing Company, 3 Park Avenue, 19th Floor, New York, New York 10016.

www.hmhco.com

Library of Congress Cataloging-in-Publication Data
Beaumont, Karen.
I like myself!/by Karen Beaumont; illustrated by David Catrow.
p. cm.
Summary: In rhyming text, a child expresses her self-esteem and exults in her unique identity.
[1. Self-esteem—Fiction.   2. Identity—Fiction.   3. Stories in rhyme.]   I. Catrow, David, ill.   II. Title.
PZ8.3.B3845Ik   2004
[E]—dc21   2002153854
ISBN-13: 978-0-15-202013-2   ISBN-10: 0-15-202013-6

SCP   25 24 23
4500591410

Printed in China

The illustrations in this book were created with watercolor, ink, pencil, and paper.
The display lettering was created by Jane Dill.
The text type was set in Minya Nouvelle.
Color separations by Bright Arts, Ltd., Hong Kong
Printed and bound in China
Production supervision by Sandra Grebenar and Ginger Boyer
Designed by Judythe Sieck

There's no one else
I'd rather be.

I like my eyes, my ears, my nose.
I like my fingers and my toes.

I like me wild.
I like me tame.
I like me different
and the same.

I like me fast. I like me slow.
I like me everywhere I go.

I like me on the inside, too,
for all I think and say and do.

Inside, outside, upside down,
from head to toe and all around,
I like it all! It all is me!
And me is all I want to be.

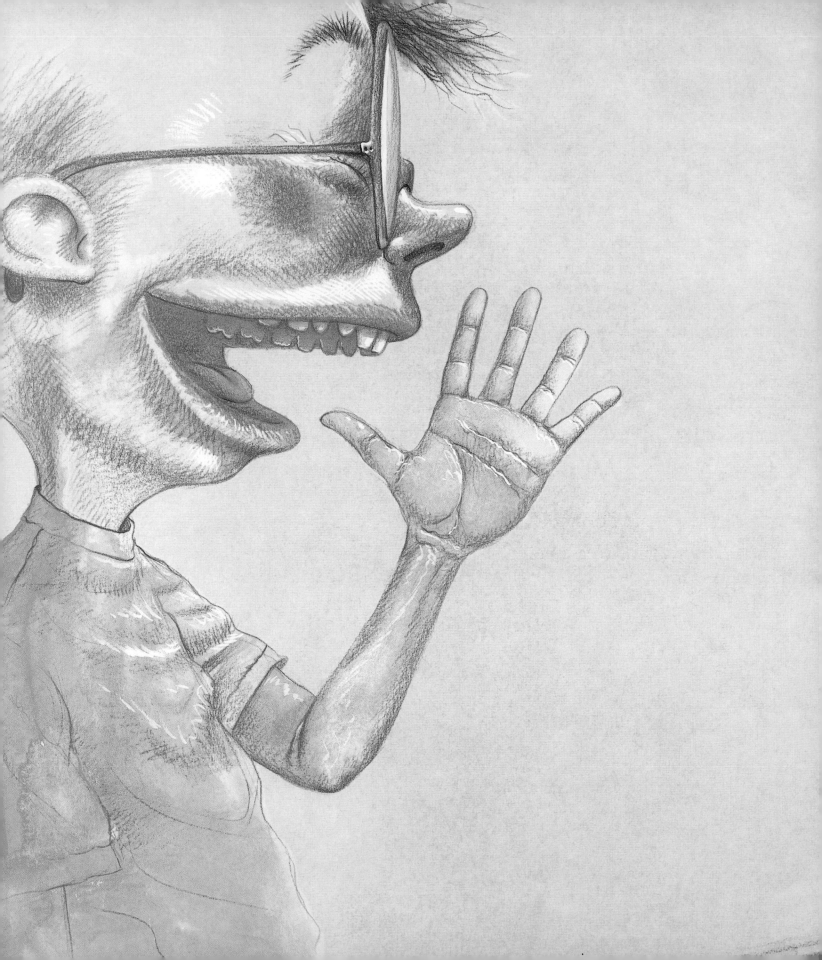

And I don't care in any way
what someone else may think or say.

I may be called a silly nut
or crazy cuckoo bird—so what?
I'm having too much fun, you see,
for anything to bother me!

Even when I look a mess,
I still don't like me any less,
'cause nothing in this world, you know,
can change what's deep inside, and so...

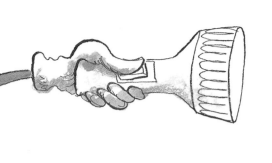

No matter if they stop and stare,
no person
ever
anywhere
can make me feel that what they see
is all there really is to me.

I'd *still* like me with fleas or warts,
or with a silly snout that snorts,

or knobby knees or hippo hips
or purple polka-dotted lips,

or beaver breath or stinky toes
or horns protruding from my nose,

or–yikes!–with spikes all down my spine,
or hair that's like a porcupine.

I *still* would be the same, you see...

I like myself because I'm **ME!**